NOV   2015

AL'S WORLD

KILLER LUNCH LADY

AL'S WORLD
KILLER LUNCH LADY

BOOK 2

Elise Leonard

ALADDIN PAPERBACKS
New York London Toronto Sydney

This book is a work of fiction. Any references to historical events, real people, or real locales are used fictitiously. Other names, characters, places, and incidents are the product of the author's imagination, and any resemblance to actual events or locales or persons, living or dead, is entirely coincidental.

ALADDIN PAPERBACKS
An imprint of Simon & Schuster Children's Publishing Division
1230 Avenue of the Americas, New York, NY 10020
Copyright © 2007 by Elise Leonard
All rights reserved, including the right of reproduction in whole or in part in any form.
ALADDIN PAPERBACKS and related logo are registered trademarks of Simon & Schuster, Inc.
Designed by Christopher Grassi
The text of this book was set in Berkeley Old Style.
Manufactured in the United States of America
First Aladdin Paperbacks edition June 2007
10 9 8 7 6 5 4 3 2 1
Library of Congress Control Number 2006936002
ISBN-13: 978-1-4169-3465-3

ACKNOWLEDGMENTS

To all the lunch ladies out there
(my mother-in-law included):
You know most of you can't cook—
but you still show up
to make food for gazillions of kids
every . . . single . . . day.

That takes guts!

For my readers:
Stick with the peanut butter cookies.
They're usually good.
And avoid the "tuna surprise" whenever possible.

For my wonderful husband John
(whose mother was a lunch lady):
One of the things I love most about you is that
no matter *how* bad dinner turns out . . .
you always eat it. Thanks!

For my sons Michael and John:
Here's a very important life lesson:
When in doubt, go for the PB&J!!!

~Elise

CHAPTER

1

"I think Mrs. Holt is a killer," Mike said.

"Me too." Keith said. He had a bag lunch, but he was looking at my food.

"Yeah," I agreed. "I know what you mean."

I looked down at my tray. Big mistake. It's best not to look at it. At least not straight on.

Lunch food. It was better just to eat it. You know, with your eyes closed.

When you looked at it, you wouldn't be hungry anymore. Any idiot knows that.

School lunch food was most edible when you had a cold. Then you couldn't smell it. Or really taste it. That's when it tasted best.

Too bad I didn't have a cold.

"What *is* this?" I asked.

I poked at my lunch.

It didn't move, so that was a good thing. The only problem was that I didn't think it should be brown. *Whatever* it was.

"I'm not talking about the food," Mike said.

"*What?* You *like* this stuff?" I asked as I poked at it again. It still didn't move.

"Of course I don't like it, Al!" Mike said. "Do I *look* like I don't have a tongue?"

We all stared at Mike.

"You look like you don't have a brain," Roshni said.

Roshni always cracked on people. No one took it to heart.

"Can you *look* like you don't have a brain?" Keith asked. "I mean, that's not something you can really *see*."

"At least not yours," Roshni said back to Keith.

Things were getting out of hand. I had to change the subject.

"I think it's meat loaf," I said.

"My brain?" Keith asked.

I wanted to say something to Keith, but knew that one Roshni in the bunch was enough.

Before Roshni could answer Keith, I spoke up. "No, the brown stuff. I think it's meat loaf."

"Would you forget about the brown stuff?" Roshni said to me. "For all we know, it's poop on a plate."

Mike threw his fork down. "Okay. Now I can't eat it. Thanks a *lot*!"

"You were going to *eat* it?" Roshni asked Mike.

"I'm so hungry, I was going to *try*."

"Here. Take my corn bread," Keith said. He held out a square of corn bread.

"Your Mom's *famous* corn bread?" Mike asked.

Keith nodded.

"Thanks!" Mike said as he snatched the corn

bread out of Keith's hand. He started eating it like he was on *Survivor* or something and hadn't eaten in days. "God, this is good," he said to Keith. He was taking huge bites.

Just then, four tables over, everyone started screaming.

A crowd formed, and Roshni ran over there.

Keith, Mike, and I stayed seated. We figured we'd wait until Roshni came back. We knew he'd tell us everything.

"That idiot—Chris Vale—shoved another Tater Top up his nose," Roshni said as he came back.

We rolled our eyes.

"Yeah, what else is new?" I said.

Chris Vale shoved a Tater Top up his nose at *least* two times a week. We think he did it to get the attention of some girl. But all he got was Mrs. Holt jumping over the lunch counter.

Mrs. Holt is the lunch lady. She's a real weirdo. And of course, she can't cook.

That's why the school hired her.

Have you ever met a lunch lady who could cook?

I can see their interviews. The school principal asks a future lunch lady to bring in a sample of her cooking. If it's totally disgusting, she gets hired. If her food is somewhere near good, she's probably told to go to a restaurant. "No use wasting your skills on *these* kids," the principal probably says.

"You know, I've never had a school lunch that was any good. In *all* my years of school," I said. I poked at the brown stuff some more.

"Yeah, me neither," Keith said. "That's why I 'bring.'"

"Can you guys forget about the food for a minute?" Mike said.

He looked worried. Or upset. I couldn't tell which.

But Keith hadn't noticed.

"We're at *lunch*, man. How can we forget about food?" Keith asked Mike.

"Because there are other things to worry about," Mike said.

"Like what?" I asked.

"Like, I think our lunch lady *really* is a killer," Mike said.

We all looked at Mike. Then we looked at Mrs. Holt.

She was walking around the lunchroom. Her eyes were wild and shifty. And she looked nervous.

"Okay. I'll bite," I said as I turned back to Mike.

"Yeah, me too," Keith said. "Why do you think she's a killer?"

"She's always doing stuff that's not, you know, very lunch ladyish," Mike alleged.

"She's weird, but that doesn't make her a killer," Roshni said.

"Yeah, if 'being weird' made you a killer, then Chris Vale would be a serial killer," I said.

"You mean a Tater Tot killer," Keith said.

"What?" Roshni asked Keith.

"You know. He's not a *cereal* killer. He's a *Tater Tot* killer," Keith said. Then he laughed.

He was the only one who laughed.

"You really are an idiot," Roshni said to Keith.

"Like take now," Mike said. "Look at her. What is she *doing?*" He got us back on topic. That was good.

She was waving some kind of metal box thing around.

CHAPTER

2

"What do you think it is?" I asked.

No one was looking at Mrs. Holt. They were all watching the nurse pull yet another Tater Tot from Chris Vale's nose.

"Oh, my God! He's *bleeding*!" Tina Link said.

The nurse held up the Tater Tot and looked at it closely.

Then she looked at Chris and shook her head. She was making a face that clearly said that she was beginning to hate her job.

Chris smiled at her and then laughed.

Whatever the joke was, the nurse didn't find it funny. I knew that because she sighed. It was so loud, I could hear it all the way over here.

"Aren't you going to *do* something?" Principal Newman asked the nurse.

"No," she said as she packed up her stuff.

"But, he's *bleeding*," Tina Link said loudly.

Everyone stopped talking and listened carefully.

Yes, we were used to Chris Vale's antics, but this "bleeding" thing was new.

Maybe he finally hurt something. Maybe Chris Vale finally shoved one too many Tater Tots where it didn't belong. Maybe he had a rupture or something. That would be cool. *Really* cool.

Maybe his head would explode from all the other stuff he must have packed up there. I mean, if he did Tater Tots at school, maybe he did something like that at home too. And there wasn't a nurse at home to go up there fishing stuff out. So it all had to be packed in there.

I could only *imagine* the strange things that were shoved up his nose canal.

We all waited quietly to hear what the nurse was going to say next.

She shook her head. "No. He's not bleeding."

"But I *saw* the blood," Mr. Newman said.

"Yeah, me too," Tina said with concern.

"Ketchup," Mrs. Poi said.

Mr. Newman stared at Chris Vale. Actually, we were *all* staring at Chris Vale.

"There is something *seriously* wrong with you, son. Keep this up and I'm going to tell your parents to get you tested," Mr. Newman said.

Keith laughed at that. "Can you *test* for stupidity?"

Roshni looked at Keith. "Isn't that what tests are *for*?"

"You're a real 'glass half empty' kind of guy, aren't you?" I said to Roshni. It was more a statement than a question.

"Look at her," Mike said softly.

He was still watching the lunch lady, Mrs. Holt.

She was waving that little metal box all around. She looked like a scarecrow waving in the wind. Or a hectic businesswoman trying to hail a cab.

It would have looked funny if it weren't so . . . bizarre.

"What *is* she doing?" Keith asked me.

I looked at my best friend. Why does he always think *I* know everything?

"I don't know, Keith. Do I *look* like her mother?" I asked him.

He shrugged. "I don't know. I've never seen her mother."

Roshni laughed. "If Al looks like Mrs. Holt's mother, then she's one butt-ugly woman."

"Can we *focus*, people?" Mike cried out. "There's something really wrong with this picture. Don't you think?"

Mrs. Holt was now running around. She looked like a chicken with her head cut off. Not that I'd ever *seen* a chicken with its head cut off. But I'd imagine it would be pretty funny.

She was sticking that metal box at each lunch table. Then she was looking at each kid. Hard. Like she was wondering if they were up to something.

"What *is* she doing?" I asked aloud.

I didn't expect an answer.

We watched as she quickly moved from table to table. She was trying to get whatever she was doing done by the time the Chris Vale chaos ended.

It *was* ending. So she was being more subtle about it. But she was still doing it. Whatever "it" was.

"Maybe she's a spy," Keith said.

I rolled my eyes. "And what's she trying to do? See how many kids get sick from her cooking?"

"Can a metal box do that?" Mike asked.

"Maybe it's a vomit meter," Keith said.

"Do they *have* a vomit meter?" Mike asked Keith. "I don't think they have vomit meters."

As stupid as it came off, Keith was sticking with

his whole "vomit meter" idea. "It's probably a high-*tech* vomit meter."

"Oh, yeah. That explains *everything*," I said. I couldn't stop my eyes from rolling.

I really liked my friends, but sometimes they were real morons.

"Well, what do *you* think she's doing?" Keith asked me.

"I don't know, for sure. But I think it's safe to say she's *not* metering vomit," I said.

Just then, Mrs. Holt passed her box thingie in front of Melissa Evans.

A little red light on the box started flashing like crazy.

"Ohhh," I said slowly. "It's a metal detector."

Everyone looked at me.

"How do you know?" Mike asked.

"When she waved it in from of Melissa Evans's face, it went ballistic," I explained.

"You mean Metal Mouth?" Roshni asked.

We all gave him a look. "That's mean," I said.

"Yeah," Keith and Mike agreed.

"Well, she *does* have some pretty heavy-duty braces," he said.

"So? It's not her fault," I argued.

Roshni ate a large spoon of his pudding. Then he spit it out and wiped his tongue with a paper napkin. Paper bits stuck to his tongue.

"Dang, that's gross!" he said. He was spitting into his napkin.

"It's pudding. How gross can it be?" Keith asked.

He took a spoonful of Roshni's pudding.

"Oh, my God! It's awful!" he said as he made a face and spit it out.

"What kind is it?" I asked.

It was yellow. So that meant it could be vanilla or banana. Or maybe even butterscotch.

"It's . . . I don't know. I've never tasted anything like it before," Roshni said.

"Tastes like chicken," Keith said.

"You think *everything* tastes like chicken," I said to Keith.

Roshni was choking and gagging. "Oh, no! Do you really think it's chicken?"

For Roshni's sake, I hoped it wasn't. He doesn't eat meat. It's a religious thing.

"Sorry, buddy, but I think it is," Keith said.

I shook my head and grabbed my spoon.

"It can't be," I muttered. "Who makes chicken pudding for dessert?"

I took a taste. Like the others, I also spit it out.

"Dang! That's the grossest thing I've *ever* tasted."

It was *far* worse than any school lunch I'd had up until that point. And like I'd said, I'd had plenty of horrible lunches.

Roshni was still wiping and spitting to get all traces of pudding from his mouth.

"If it *is* chicken, will you go to hell now?" Keith asked Roshni.

"We don't believe in hell," Roshni said. "But in my *next* life, I'll probably come back as a . . ." Roshni was thinking.

"A what?" Mike asked.

"I don't know. I was trying to think what I would come back as that was worse than I already am. But I can't think of anything."

"That's pathetic," I said to Roshni.

"Yeah. Tell me about it," he said.

Just then, Mrs. Holt stuck her metal box thing at our table.

"If that's a vomit meter, we'll probably read pretty high," Keith said to her.

"Excuse me?" she said.

"We just had your pudding," Mike said.

You'd think she'd be offended by that. But she wasn't. She just laughed.

"I added chicken stock instead of banana flavoring by mistake," she said.

"You *knew* that?" Keith asked.

"And you *still* served it anyhow?" Roshni asked.

He looked shocked.

"Yes, well, it was getting late by the time I figured out my mistake. And I didn't have another dessert made. And lunchtime was almost here. So I had to serve it."

"Chicken pudding," Mike said. His face said it all.

She shrugged. "Sorry, guys."

She didn't look sorry. And she acted like it was no big deal.

"I don't eat meat," Roshni said to her. "For religious reasons."

Now she looked sorry.

She looked at Roshni. "I'm truly sorry."

He shrugged, but he didn't tell her it was okay.

"What's your name again?" she asked him.

"Roshni. Roshni Mageed."

She nodded. "Okay, Roshni. From now on, if I make a mistake like that, I'll come to you and will let you know."

"Are you *planning* to make more mistakes like that?" Mike asked.

It sounded like she did.

"Well, I hope not. But I can't guarantee anything," she said.

Those weren't really the words I was hoping to hear.

"I kind of stink as a lunch lady," she said with a laugh.

That was a strange thing to say.

"Yeah, no kidding," Roshni said.

"Killed anyone yet?" Mike asked her.

He was still obviously still stuck on the "our lunch lady is a killer" thought.

She looked at Mike, and when he kept staring at her, she winked.

"To be honest, I've killed a few people. But don't worry. Not with my cooking," she said with a grin.

"So what are you doing with a metal detector?" I asked her.

Her grin left quickly. A mean scowl took its place.

Her face was a mask of anger and hatred. But only for a second.

And then it was gone.

For that split second, I got scared.

"It's just a hobby of mine," she said lightly. "It relaxes me."

She was now smiling again.

"Some people like looking for coins on a beach. I do this," she said right before she walked away.

CHAPTER

3

"What was *that* all about?" Keith asked.

"I told you there was something wrong with her," Mike said. "She's a nutcase! I still think she's a killer."

"She was just playing with us," I said. "Right, guys?" I asked nervously.

I mean, maybe I was the only one who'd just gotten freaked out.

Maybe I was the only one who thought she'd turned evil for a second there.

"I don't know," Roshni said. "She seemed pretty serious."

"Yeah. And she has the eyes of a killer," Mike said.

We all looked at Mike.

"What's *that* supposed to mean?" I asked.

"It means she has the eyes of a killer."

Just then she came back.

"Oh, and Roshni?" she said to Roshni. "If it makes you feel better, I doubt there's any real chicken in the chicken stock. It's probably a cheap substitute. You know, all chemicals. Nothing real. It would cost a lot more if it were real. So you're probably safe."

Cheap substitute? Chemicals? That sounded grosser than if it *were* real chicken stock.

I guess they figured whatever didn't kill us made us stronger.

I turned to Keith. "If you notice that I'm starting to grow another arm out of my neck or something, let me know. Okay? That's when I'll know I should really start bringing a bag lunch."

"You should probably start bringing a bag lunch anyhow," Mrs. Holt said. "Even if you don't grow that arm from your neck. My cooking really *is* bad."

"So why'd you get a job as a school lunch lady? You know, if you can't cook?" Mike asked her suspiciously.

She was about to answer him when she saw Beth Smith get up from her table.

Beth looked at Mrs. Holt and made a hand signal.

Wow. If I'd done that to my mother, I would have been grounded.

If I'd done that to a teacher, I would have been suspended.

If I'd done that to, say, an upperclassman, I would have been punched.

But Beth Smith did it to Mrs. Holt. And nothing happened to her. What was up with that?

And clomping right behind Beth was Diane Simpson. Beth's best friend. They were headed for the door.

"I'm out of here," Beth hissed to Mrs. Holt as she passed by.

"Yeah. We're outta here," Diane said.

"And don't try to stop me," Beth said between clenched teeth.

Mrs. Holt looked shocked. And then nervous.

She looked around. All around. She looked at the door. She looked at Beth. She looked at the door again. Then she looked at me.

"Al," she said.

"What?" I asked.

"You've got to do me a favor," she said.

Was she nuts? *Me?* Do *her* a favor?

I said nothing.

"Look, I don't have time to explain. You need to do this for me," she said.

"First off, I don't know what 'this' is. And second off, I don't *have* to do *anything* for you," I said. "You're just the lunch lady. It's not like you give me a grade or anything."

"Yeah, you can't even make us a good lunch!

Why should we do anything for you?" Roshni said. I guess he was still mad about the chicken pudding.

"If we had to give you a grade, I'm sorry, Mrs. Holt, but it would probably be a D," Keith said.

"More like an F," Roshni added.

Mrs. Holt looked at the door. "I don't have time for this, guys. I need your help, and I need it now."

Beth and Diane were leaving. She looked frantic.

I kind of felt sorry for her.

"What is it?" I asked. "What's the favor?"

"I need you to follow Beth and Diane. But mostly Beth," she said.

"Why?" Mike asked.

"I can't tell you," she said.

Mike was always nervous about stuff like that. He was a worrywart. "Then I can't do it," Mike said.

Mrs. Holt looked at me. "What about you, Al?"

I shrugged. "I don't know."

"I'll get you a pass out of all of your classes," she offered.

"I'm in!" I said quickly. I didn't want her to take back her offer.

"Me too!" Keith said. "Can I get a pass too?"

Mrs. Holt smiled briefly. "Yeah, sure, Keith."

"Well, I can't do it," Roshni said. "I have a science test next period. And I studied for it. I don't want to miss it. I'll get a hundred on it, I know."

I looked at Mrs. Holt. "Well, me and Keith are in. You just want us to follow them?" I asked her.

"Yes. And call me with updates. I need to know where Beth is at all times."

Mrs. Holt looked around. She grabbed a pen out of her apron thingie. But she didn't have a piece of paper.

She grabbed my hand and pulled it to her. Then she wrote her number on the back of my arm. It went down my wrist. One number went on the back of my hand.

She was writing with a felt-tip marker and it tickled. I giggled.

"This is serious, Al. You can't fool around. Or mess this up," she said gravely.

I scratched my head. "Okay, Mrs. Holt. Where's the pass?" I asked.

"Just go. I'll straighten it out with all of your teachers. Just go now and try to find her. And then—don't lose her."

"Okay," I said.

"And don't forget to call me on my cell phone," she said. She nodded at my arm.

"Okay," I said.

"Check in regularly," she added.

"Okay," I said. "Don't you want us to go now?"

"Yes. Go," she said as she pushed me toward the door.

And there it was . . . freedom.

At least I thought it was "freedom." But I was terribly wrong.

Oh, so terribly wrong!

CHAPTER
4

Keith and I followed Beth and Diane from school to the mall.

They almost lost us a few times, but we kept up with them.

You can't *imagine* what girls do with their time. It's freaky!

They went into *every single* clothing shop in the mall. They tried on just about everything in each store. Every single piece of clothing in every single store.

Oh yeah, and I bet you're wondering what they bought. Right?

Well, they bought . . . *nothing*!

It was a *total* waste of time.

Then they looked at jewelry. Tons and *tons* of jewelry!

And did they buy any of *that*? No.

It was hard not to compare girls and guys. We guys are so different.

First off, we don't go into a store unless we *want* something.

Then we look around until we find it.

Finally, we actually *buy* it!

And after that? We leave.

There's none of this "window shopping." Or "just looking around." Well, except for cars. And maybe video games.

But besides that? It's just: We know what we want, we get in, we buy it, and we get out!

"What are *you* doing here?" Beth asked me.

I hadn't noticed that she'd noticed me. I was too busy being turned off by her shopping ritual.

"I . . . ah . . . I . . ." I looked at Keith. I choked. I had nothing.

"We're looking for a gift," Keith said.

Oh, that was good. Really smooth. I was impressed.

"For your girlfriend?" Diane asked me.

That made Keith crack up. "Ha! *Al?* With a *girl-friend?*"

I elbowed him in the ribs. "It's not that strange a concept," I said to him.

But it was too late to say I had a girlfriend. Keith had already ruined *that* cover! "No, it's for my mother. It's her birthday."

Sure, I was lying. But then I figured that if it was anywhere *near* my mother's birthday, I wouldn't be lying. The problem was, I had no idea when my mother's birthday was.

Heck, it *could* have been tomorrow, for all I knew. For that matter, it could be today!

Then I felt guilty for missing my mother's birth-day if it *was* today.

I shook my head to clear it. No, it probably wasn't today. The odds of that were like one in seven or something.

"What are you thinking about getting her?" Beth asked.

I looked around.

To my right was the ladies underwear department. My eyes flew to a bright pink bra.

Nooooo. Not that.

My gaze shifted to the left.

Watches.

Yeah. That was good. A watch. "I thought a watch would be nice," I said.

"That *would* be nice," Keith said. He sounded surprised.

I gave him a look. "What? You don't think I can pick out something nice for my mother?" I asked him. I was getting mad.

"Well, honestly? No."

I was about to pop him when he said, "Remember

last year? You bought her a crocheted toilet paper roll cover."

"It was 'girly.' I thought she'd like it," I said. "And I got it at a crafts fair. So it was handmade. I thought that would make it extra nice."

Keith sighed loudly. "Mothers like it when it's homemade when *you* make it, Al. Not when some eighty-nine-year-old, half-blind spinster makes it."

"Well, it was so poorly made, I thought my mother would *think* I made it!"

"You crochet?" Diane asked me. Her face looked like she'd just sucked a lemon.

"No I don't *crochet*, Diane," I said.

Now I was defending my manhood? This was getting out of hand. Totally out of hand.

"Do you guys want to help me pick out a watch? Or what?" I asked gruffly.

"Yeah, sure. But we have to leave to go to the movies soon," Diane said. She looked at Beth to make sure she was correct.

"Yes. We have to leave soon to go to the movies."

"That's okay," I said. "We're going to the movies too," I added. I looked at Keith and gave him the eye.

"We are?" he said.

I stared at him. "Yeah. We are. That's why we cut school. *Remember?*" I asked him.

"I thought we cut school to follow—" Then his hand clamped over his mouth. His big, *stupid* mouth.

"That's right," I cut in quickly. "We left school to follow my lifelong dream to buy my mother a nice watch."

I looked at the girls. They were looking at me and smiling.

"That's so sweet," Beth said.

"Yeah, it *is* kind of sweet," Diane added. "I always thought you were a real dork. But that's kind of sweet."

I don't know why, but I blushed. "Yeah, well," I stammered. "My mom deserves a nice watch. She's been putting up with me for my entire lifetime. She deserves it."

I didn't think I said anything funny, but the girls giggled.

We looked at the watches. The saleslady was helping a lady who looked like she had a lot of money, so she never came over our way.

"We'd better go to our movie," Beth said, "or we'll miss it."

I gave Keith a look.

"Us too," he said.

"We can always come back after the movie to get the watch," I said. "I'd be happy if you'd help me. I really don't know much about what stuff is worth."

Keith laughed. "And he's so cheap, he *hates* to get ripped off."

The girls giggled again.

"Okay. We'll help you. After the movie," Beth said.

If the girls hadn't said they'd help me, I would

have belted Keith. He was being a real pain in the butt! And I didn't like the way he kept trying to make me look bad.

Well, maybe he wasn't *trying* to make me look bad. But the things he was saying sure *did* make me look bad.

Even if they were all true.

"We're going to see *The Princess Takes a Prince*. What movie are you guys going to see?" Diane asked.

"There's a great new Vin Diesel movie out," Keith said to me.

The kid was a real half-wit.

"I wanted to see *The Princess Takes a Prince*," I said.

Keith looked more grossed out than Roshni did when he ate the chicken pudding. He looked more grossed out then Roshni did when Roshni found out it *was* chicken pudding.

"You *do*?" Keith asked me. "You actually *want* to see *The Princess Takes a Prince*?"

Keith choked on the words. It would've been funny if he weren't being such a stupid idiot!

I mean, we were there to *follow* the girls. Why would we go to a *different* movie from theirs? Wouldn't it be easier to follow them if we went to the *same* movie?

"Are you crazy, Keith? You *know* I love the 'Princess' movies," I said.

"You do?" Diane asked me. Once again she looked like she'd just sucked a lemon.

My macho-ness was really taking a beating today.

"Yeah, I do. Do you have a problem with that?" I asked her.

She shrugged. "I guess not, "she said.

"I guess you're in touch with your feminine side," Beth said to me.

Keith was cracking up. But he was a moron. Because if he could see how she was looking at me, he wouldn't be laughing.

CHAPTER

5

Keith and I got popcorn and sodas. The girls asked us to get the snacks while they went to the ladies' room. Beth gave me a huge wad of money.

"I can't believe you're making me see *The Princess Takes a Prince*," Keith whined.

"Oh, buck up, Keith," I said. "It's a movie. You'll see it, you'll leave. Big deal."

"I guess," he said. His shoulders sagged.

"It'll all be over in two hours," I said. I smiled and patted him on the back.

The girls came back from the ladies' room. I reached into my pocket and gave Beth her change from the snacks, plus the rest of her money.

"Thanks for getting the snacks," she said.

"Thanks for paying," I said back to her.

She smiled. "It's nothing."

Yeah. I bet it was nothing. With a wad of money like that, who cares if you spend five bucks for a popcorn and soda?

The next thing Beth said was *really* weird. She turned to Diane and said, "You sit with him, okay?" Beth was nodding toward Keith.

Diane didn't look happy. "Why? Because we're both black?" she asked with a huff.

Beth leaned over to Diane and whispered into her ear.

Diane made a face, giggled, and looked at me.

"You can *have* him," she said to Beth. Then she turned to Keith and took his arm.

Keith looked like he was about to pass out. I couldn't tell if he was happy or scared. If I had to place money on it, though, I'd go with "scared."

What Diane said wasn't the nicest thing anyone had ever said about me, but I was pleased that Beth seemed to want me. First, because it would make my job easier. And second, because it was, well, kind of nice to be wanted. Or chosen. Or whatever.

Maybe I was just the best of the worst. You know, with Keith and all.

But that thought was bringing me down. So I stuck with the "she chose me" thought.

"If you'll excuse me, I need to use the men's room," I said to Beth.

Wow. Listen to me. I sounded just like James Bond.

I sure was a classy guy.

I felt so classy, I even washed my hands after I, um, finished.

After that, we all walked to the theater and chose seats.

The place was pretty much deserted, so we could sit anywhere we wanted.

The movie started, and after a while, I had to admit, it wasn't so bad. I was even getting a little into it. Okay, maybe a lot into it.

About a half hour into the movie, I excused myself again.

I really didn't want to leave the movie, but I had to call Mrs. Holt. I'd promised.

I'm sure Beth must have thought I had a bladder problem or something. But I *really* had to call Mrs. Holt. A promise is a promise. I had to tell her where we were.

On the way out of the movie theater, I asked Keith for a quarter.

"What for?" he asked loudly.

Great. Break my cover, Keith. And make me look like an idiot.

"To make a call," I said. I was trying to be cool, but Keith was making me look stupid.

"Who ya calling?" he asked.

I noticed that he wasn't grabbing in his pants to get me that quarter. He probably wouldn't until I told him who I was calling. It was the way he was.

It was the way things were.

I was always broke. *He* was always nosy.

"I'm going to call my mother," I said. "Is that all right with you?" I hissed. "I don't want her to worry."

Beth overheard. "That's so sweet," she said. She handed me a quarter. "Here, Al."

I had my pride, so I didn't take it at first.

Then I looked at Keith. He wasn't giving up a quarter. So I looked back at Beth and smiled with shame. "Sorry. I left my wallet at home," I said to her.

Keith thought that was hilarious.

Okay. So I *never* had my wallet. And I *never* carried money. But that could be because . . . I didn't *have* any.

I shot him a look, but I didn't think he saw it. It was too dark in the movie theater.

"Thank you," I said to Beth as I took the quarter.

"No problem," she said. She smiled sweetly.

I went outside to the lobby and found a pay phone. I stuck the quarter in and held up my arm so I could see the number Mrs. Holt had written there. I started dialing the number. Then I realized, I was one number short. Dang!

I must've washed it off when I washed my hands.

See? I *knew* there was no good reason to purposely wash your hands.

I tried to read the number, but it was totally gone. Vanished.

I couldn't see the missing number at all.

Great.

I only had the one quarter, so I had to guess.

I tried to remember it.

I closed my eyes.

I kept thinking it was a seven, so I tried that.

Bingo.

"Al, is that you?" Mrs. Holt said.

"Yeah," I said. "We're in the mall. At the movies. I don't know where we'll be after that."

"Okay. Good work," she said. "Call to tell me if you go anywhere else."

"All right," I said. "I'd better get back in there."

She didn't say good-bye or anything. She just hung up.

So I walked back in to the theater.

"How's your mom?" Beth asked.

"Oh, just fine," I said.

Keith looked at me and laughed. The idiot still had no clue who I was calling. I figured he'd figure it out in the time I was gone. But, no. He didn't.

Well, I *was* talking about Keith here.

The movie ended. The Princess got her man, and the girls were all crying.

"Why are you crying?" Keith asked Diane. He looked annoyed.

She sniffled a few times. "Because I'm so happy," she said. "And the wedding was so beautiful." She blew her nose loudly. "Didn't you think the wedding was beautiful?" she asked Keith.

I saw him shrug. "I don't know. It was okay."

Keith looked at me as if to say, "Get me out of here!"

The lights came back on, and I noticed we were the only guys in the whole place.

I also noticed that we were the only ones with dry eyes too.

Chick flicks. They love leaving the ladies bawling.

"So," I said to Beth. "That was nice."

Okay. I *know* I sounded stupid. But she seemed to like it when I sounded stupid.

"Yes," she said. "Very nice."

Then she took hold of my hand.

At first it sort of freaked me out. But then I got used to it after a few seconds.

I was also glad I'd washed my hands.

"We're just going to go to the ladies' room," Beth said to me. Then she let go of my hand and took Diane's hand.

Guess she liked holding hands.

I bet her mother was happy when *she* was a little girl.

When I was a baby, my mother had to wrestle me to get me to hold hands every time we crossed a street. I hated it! But with Beth . . . it wasn't so bad.

But, she isn't my mother.

And I'm not three anymore.

As soon as they were out of earshot, I grabbed Keith.

"Keith," I said.

"What?" he asked as he looked with longing at the movie poster starring Vin Diesel.

"I washed off part of Mrs. Holt's number. But I remembered it. So I called her," I said.

"You mean you weren't calling your mother?" he said with a smile.

"No, you idiot. I went out to call Mrs. Holt."

"I *knew* you weren't going to call your mother. You never call your mother. Plus, I was thinking, why would you call your mother when you were supposed to be in school?"

I shook my head. "*That's* what you were thinking while I was gone?"

"Yeah. What did you *think* I was thinking?"

"I thought you were thinking that I was calling Mrs. *Holt*," I said with frustration.

"Now why would you do that if you washed off part of her number?" he asked.

I was ready to hit him. "You didn't know until just *now* that I'd washed off her number."

"Well, *you* didn't know then either," he said with a huff.

My hands balled into fists.

"We're ba-ack," Beth said as she and Diane walked toward us.

Keith was saved in the nick of time. I was *really* just about to pop him one. *Man*, he could be a pain in the butt! You know the saying that someone's "not working on all six cylinders"? Well, Keith's not working on two! And that's being kind. In reality, he's working on about one and a half.

Beth took my hand again.

"Let's go get your mom that watch," she said.

CHAPTER

6

We were looking at the case of watches.

"That one's nice," Diane said.

She was pointing to a glittery one with diamonds all around it. It also had diamonds for the numbers.

"I don't know," I said honestly. "It's not really my mom. If you know what I mean."

"Yeah," Keith said. "His mom's real plain."

I hit Keith in the chest. "She's not plain," I said. "She's just not fancy."

"She sounds like an M&M," Beth said.

"Oh, Eminem. I *love* him!" Diane gushed.

Were girls always this scattered? I mean, one second we're talking about a watch for my mother. Then, before I know what's going on, we're talking about music. I looked at Keith.

He shrugged.

Guess he was thinking the same thing.

"I like this one," Beth said. She was pointing to a perfect watch. It was gold, had big numbers, and was sort of pretty. My mom would love it.

"Yeah," I said. "That's the one."

"I guess so," Diane said without spirit. I think she was a little upset that we didn't all go for her diamond "bling" choice.

"That one's perfect for Al's mom," Keith said.

Then Beth said something really strange. She said, "Then so it shall be."

The saleslady was off helping another lady. She was the same saleslady as before we went to the movies. But the lady buying the jewelry was different.

"I think the saleslady likes older women," Keith said.

"Why?" I asked.

"Because this is the second time we're here and she's still ignoring us," Keith explained.

"That will not do," Beth said.

Her voice sounded different. It was like she thought she was the princess from the movie. I guess she was really into that movie. Because by the way she was now acting, you'd think she *was* a princess.

The next thing Beth did was clap her hands three times, *loudly*. Then she said, "We need your attention. *Now!*"

I couldn't believe my ears. It was so weird! "Calm down, Beth," I said.

She looked at me.

She even *looked* different now. I can't describe it.

"I will *not* calm down. I am tired of that woman's insubordination." She was pointing to the saleslady.

"Her *what?*" I asked. I had no idea what she was

talking about. Mostly because I had no idea what that word meant.

But I could tell it didn't mean something good.

"Her rudeness is *not* acceptable," Beth said. She now sounded really uppity.

I looked at Keith. He was standing there staring at Beth. I guess he didn't know what the heck she was talking about either.

Diane, on the other hand, was smiling. Like she knew what was coming.

"That lady had better look out," Diane said. She was looking at the saleslady.

"Why?" I asked her.

"Because Beth's getting ticked off."

I looked at Beth. She looked totally different to me now. Gone was the nice, easygoing girl. In her place was a person who looked . . . I don't know . . . majestic. Like royalty or something.

If you asked me, I'd probably tell you that Beth needed to stay away from the Princess movies. She was becoming just like one.

"It's okay, Beth," I said. "I don't have any money anyhow. Remember?"

She looked over at the saleslady. "We need assistance. *Right now!*" Beth ordered. Then she turned to me.

"Yes, I remember that you left your wallet at home, Al," she said to me. "I will loan you the money."

Oh. Wow. That was nice.

"Yeah," Diane said as she looked at me. "How *were* you going to buy your mom a watch if you left your wallet home?"

Before I could answer, the glass case we were standing in front of . . . exploded.

Glass flew everywhere. A piece sliced through my pants, just missing my leg.

"Are you okay?" I asked Beth. She had a shard of glass sticking out of her belt.

Her gaze followed mine and she plucked the glass from the leather belt. "Yes. That was close," she said as she threw the glass piece to the ground.

"There she is!" a man shouted from the complete other side of the store. "*Get* her!"

That's when all heck broke loose.

Guys came running toward us. The store alarms went off. Diane screamed like a lunatic. Then Beth shouted, *"Run for your lives!"*

Run for my *life*?

Ah, no offense, but Coach White would tell you that I couldn't run for my life if my *life* depended upon it. He was my gym teacher. And he knew the truth. In fact, he often said I ran worse than a girl. Which was kind of stupid. Because everyone knows that some girls can *really* run!

I knew he was just trying to get me to run faster. But that never worked. Because what he *didn't* know was that I *was* always running as fast as I could. Even when he said those mean things.

So I guess it was true.

Not that I ran like a girl. But that I couldn't run to save my life if my life depended upon it.

Because right now it seemed . . . my life *did* depend on it.

And as much as I really wanted to run like the wind . . .

I couldn't.

And it wasn't like I was going too slow or anything.

At the moment, my legs weren't moving. At *all*.

Coach was right: I *couldn't* run if my life depended upon it.

And apparently . . . it did.

CHAPTER

7

"Come on, Al, we've got to get out of here!" Keith said.

He grabbed my shirt and started pulling.

I heard a gunshot. It broke another jewelry case.

Women were screaming, and babies were crying. Alarms were blaring. I could hear sirens off in the distance.

It was total chaos.

For me, the saddest sounds were the babies crying.

"Al," Beth screamed. "Move! *Now!*"

There was something in the way she said it that made me snap out of my frozen state.

I looked at Keith and Diane. And then at Beth.

She grabbed my hand and tugged. "We've got to get *out* of here," she said.

The guys were coming toward us. There was a lot between them and us. Like ladies and strollers. And miles of clothing. And racks of purses, and other stuff the store had displayed.

As we ran from the store, Beth kept knocking displays over as soon as we'd passed them.

I kept thinking, *Eww, she's going to get into trouble for doing that.* But then I'd remember that we were being chased by guys with guns. So then I'd think, *Who cares if she knocked over some displays?*

I mean, her life was in danger too.

I didn't have time to stop and chat. But if I did, I'd probably ask her why we were running.

Oh yeah, and who those guys were.

That was a good question.

It was certainly on *my* mind.

At the moment, both Keith and Beth were dragging me along with them.

I probably would have told them to go on without me. I mean, I was only slowing them down.

I was the slow guy. The sack of potatoes. The guy everyone wished hadn't come along.

If I hadn't promised Mrs. Holt that I'd stick with Beth, I would've told them to leave me behind.

But I couldn't. Like I said. A promise is a promise.

I had to stay to follow Beth.

Even if that meant I was the guy everyone else had to carry.

One line from somewhere kept popping into my head. "Feets, don't fail me now!"

Not that mine ever did anything *but* fail me. But it could be worse. At least I was no longer frozen with fear.

For now, I was doing okay. Holding my own. Going with the flow.

And speaking of flow, the guys with the guns were gaining on us.

I may be the slowest-footed guy in our bunch, but I was probably the quickest witted. Well, at least between me and Keith.

The girls were probably smarter than me. I think Beth was even in *advanced* classes.

But, anyhow, the point is, I was the one most familiar with this town.

Diane moved here a few years ago. And Beth? She only moved here, like, last year or something.

We tore out of the store's front entrance. Right into the mall.

When we were about ten feet away from the store entrance, we heard another gunshot.

People screamed. Everyone hit the floor. So we looked a little obvious.

You know, because we were still standing.

Well, not really standing. More like running.

We were running like maniacs down the mall.

I checked out the scene behind me.

The guys with the guns were jumping over bodies to get to us.

"Quick," I said. "Turn right."

We ran toward the food court.

When we got to the Ben & Jerry's booth, I told everyone to go in there.

We hopped over the counter.

"Hi, Al," Mr. Ivan said. He looked a little taken back that we were behind the counter.

"Hey, Mr. Ivan," I said. "We're just passing through."

"Oh, okay," he said.

Mr. Ivan was always polite. He was from Russia. And had to be at *least* 150 years old.

"I'm sorry about this, Mr. Ivan," I said.

"Sorry about what?" he asked.

I reached over to his blender and pressed a button. The machine stopped whizzing. I picked up the glass container, then I poured the milk shake he was making onto the floor.

"About that," I said as I handed him back the

glass container. "Move it," I yelled to Beth, Keith, and Diane as I followed them through the long, skinny store.

"How do we get out of here?" I shouted to Mr. Ivan.

"The back door," he said, and pointed. "It leads to the mall's service entrance."

"Thanks," I called back over my shoulder.

Just then we heard a guy scream, "Whoa-oa-oa."

I looked over my shoulder again, and there was the lead bad guy, flat on his back. He was lying in a pool of icy cold milk shake.

"That ought to cool him down," I said to my friends.

Diane let out a little laugh. It was a nervous laugh. I could tell.

We made it to the back door. Diane threw it open.

I heard another thud. Another bad guy was sprawled out on the floor. This time, facedown.

"Keep running," I yelled.

I was pleased that my clever trick worked.

I knew it would, because I once dropped a Ben & Jerry's milk shake on the floor. When the mall's cleaning service guy came by to clean it up, he didn't see it. It was a vanilla shake on a white tile floor.

Anyhow, the guy slipped and fell with a *splat* right in the shake.

I felt so bad that I walked over to him to help him out.

When I reached to grab his hand and pull him up, I also slipped and fell with a *splat*. Right into the messy milk shake.

We looked like the Three Stooges. Only minus a Stooge.

Well, until Keith came along.

Then we were the Three Stooges! Because he fell in too.

I wondered if Keith was thinking the same thing I was thinking.

"Remember when you dropped your shake?" Keith asked me as we ran like idiots.

I guess he *was* thinking what I was thinking.

Just then we broke out of the mall's back entrance.

The sun was bright and hurt my eyes. It was only about three o'clock or so, but there were no clouds, so the sun was strong.

"Go left," I shouted.

"Why?" Beth asked. Her voice was strained. She was getting winded.

"The train station," I said.

We kept running until we hit the station.

We ran up to the information booth. They also sold tickets there.

"When's the next train out of here?" I asked the man behind the glass wall.

He looked at us over his half-glasses.

Then he pursed his lips like he'd tasted something really bad. "That would be the three-ten special, leaving on track B."

"We'll take four tickets," Beth said in that high-and-mighty voice she'd started using after the movie.

"Please," I added, just to be polite.

I smiled at the man, who looked bored and *very* tired.

"Don't you want to know where it's going?" he asked Beth.

"Not particularly," she answered.

"I do," Keith said to the man.

All of a sudden, Diane screamed. "They're *coming!*"

I looked out the train station's glass door.

"We'll take four tickets," Beth said. She handed him a few large bills from her big wad of money. "And you can keep the change. But only if you do *not* mention that you saw us—to *anyone.*"

The man looked at the bills. There were two that I saw that had two zeros on them. I don't know how much she'd paid the guy. Or how much the tickets cost. But she'd just given him at *least* two hundred dollars.

The weird thing was that her wad of money looked just as big as it had before.

I wondered how much could be there.

But before I could wrap my mind around the huge number, she grabbed my shirt and tugged me toward the tracks.

CHAPTER

We found track A and then track B.

"This is it," Beth said as she pulled me onto the train on track B.

Keith and Diane were right behind us.

There was a whole gaggle of nuns on the train. It looked like a penguin convention.

They were all talking and laughing and bobbing around all over the place.

All I heard was stuff like, "Sister Clara? Where are you, Sister Clara?"

"Over here, Sister Mona."

"Where, Sister Clara?" Sister Mona asked.

"Right here, Sister Mona," Sister Clara said back.

"I can't see you, Sister Clara," Sister Mona said.

For goodness' sake! Was it any *wonder* Sister Mona couldn't find Sister Clara? They all looked alike!

But I have good hearing, so I knew which one was Sister Clara.

"Excuse me, please," I said to Beth. I pried my shirt from her hand.

I grabbed Sister Mona's hand and dragged her over to Sister Clara.

"There you go," I said to Sister Mona. I nodded at Sister Clara.

Sister Mona smiled widely. "Thank you, dear boy," Sister Mona said. "It was like finding a needle in a haystack."

"Any time, Sister," I said with a smile.

Just then I saw the bad guys. They were walking

along the tracks, looking in the train windows.

I don't think Beth, Keith, or Diane saw. First off, because they were gawking at all the nuns and not looking behind them. And second off, because they weren't freaking out.

I, on the other hand, *saw* the guys. And *was* freaking out.

"Um, Sisters?" I said.

I was talking to Sister Mona and Sister Clara, but everyone seemed to stop talking, and turned to me.

Oh well, at least I had their attention.

"We're, um, being chased by bad guys with guns. And, um, I know it's probably a sin and everything. But do you think you could hide us until the train leaves?"

Like lightning, the old girls flew into motion.

Black fabric was flying all over the place.

It was like a big blur.

Women were chattering like mad. They were making a real racket. It was worse than a gaggle of geese when it was time to take off for Florida for the winter.

Before I knew what hit me, I was standing right in the middle of a bunch of gabby nuns.

I was also wearing . . . a full nun's habit.

You know. Long black dress. Long, black-and-white hat. Long, silver cross. A bunch of beads. And all.

I looked down at myself. Oh, this was bad.

I didn't go to church much. But there was one thing I knew for sure: This *had* to be a sin.

Posing as a nun.

There was no amount of Hail Marys one could do to get *that* sin off your back.

I looked down at myself.

Oh, yeah. It was official. I was going to hell. I could *feel* it.

I tried to find Keith.

I looked all around, but didn't see him.

I *did* hear him.

He was cracking up like a hyena.

"You look *wack*, Al!" he said. "You are one butt-ugly nun." Then he turned to the sisters around him. "No offense, Sisters."

"None taken," Sister Mona said to Keith.

Then she looked at me. "You really *are* one butt-ugly nun."

All the nuns started laughing, like this was a party or something.

That's when the guys poked their heads into our train's door.

Of course I couldn't take my eyes off the doorway. But the nuns were laughing and playing, and chattering like old hens.

I didn't know if Sister Mona had planned it that way. But it sure did work out perfectly. Because the bad guy nodded his head briefly as he looked around.

Then he apologized for barging in, and left.

He moved on to the next train car.

"Oh, that was *fun*," Sister Mona said.

I was sweating up whoever's habit I was wearing. For me, that was *far* from "fun."

"Glad you enjoyed it," I said to Sister Mona. I started to take off the habit.

"No, wait," Sister Mona said. "You should leave it on. Just in case they come back."

Oh. Yeah. Right.

Great.

Keith laughed at me again. "God, you're ugly," he said to me.

"Knock it off, or I'll deck you," I said to my best friend.

"Now, that's not very sisterly of you, Al," he said back.

I'd warned him.

I reached up quickly and was about to punch him when my cross went flying up and hit me in the face. It stopped me in my tracks.

I put my fist down.

Sister Mona was standing there, smiling at me.

"There's a lot of responsibility that goes with the outfit," she said. She said it quietly so only I could hear her.

I felt ashamed and nodded. "I'm sorry, Sister," I said.

"It's okay, Al," she said. "I would have knocked his socks off too."

That surprised me.

"When I was *your* age, of course," she added.

I nodded. "Of course."

I looked at Keith, who was still wearing a grin on his face that I wanted to knock off.

I rose to my fullest height. Then I spoke to him.

I looked him in the eye and seriously said, "We are *all* beautiful."

I was acting as if I were a bigwig or something. You know. Someone of importance. Not just a kid who wanted to deck his best friend.

"Very well said, Al," Sister Mona said with a warm smile.

"Yes," Sister Clara added. "Very nice sentiment."

"Thank you," I said to them both. I felt proud.

"You are a wise boy, Al," Sister Mona said. "Why are you in trouble, son?"

Keith started laughing. "Al? *Wise?* That's a laugh."

The look Sister Mona gave Keith shut him right up.

Wow. Cool.

"I don't like your ways, young man," she said to Keith. "We treat everyone with respect in this family."

I could tell what Keith was thinking. He was thinking, *I'm not part of your family.*

But I guess in the big scheme of things, we were *all* part of the same family.

And I think Keith came to the same conclusion.

"I'm sorry, Sister Mona," he said.

He really looked sorry.

"Don't tell *me*," she said to Keith. "Tell *him*." She nodded her head at me.

"Sorry, bud," Keith said to me.

"It's okay," I said.

"This is all very nice, Sisters," Beth said. "But my friends and I really should get out of here."

Sister Mona looked at Beth. Her head tilted slightly. Then something came to her. I could tell. It was as if Sister Mona suddenly recognized Beth. Which was strange.

"Why do you have to leave, dear?" Sister Mona asked Beth.

"Because men are after us. I mean, me. Men are after me," Beth answered.

"Yeah," I said to Beth. "Why *are* they after you?"

The conductor announced that the train was leaving soon.

Sister Mona waved my question off and turned to Beth.

"What better cover than to travel with us as nuns?" Sister Mona asked.

Cover? Sister Mona knew about traveling under-*cover*?

Sister Mona was turning out to be one cool nun. And, personally, I didn't know there *were* any of those. You know, cool nuns.

Not that I'd actually known many.

"Well, one *big* problem is that . . . ," Keith stammered, "Al and I are *guys*."

"Yes, Keith, we already know that," Sister Mona said.

She looked at him without any readable expression. "We may be nuns, but we're not *idiots*."

I had to laugh. "You're pretty cool, Sister," I said to Sister Mona.

"Thanks, Al," she said. "I think you're pretty cool too. Even while in a dress."

Keith cracked up and smiled at Sister Mona.

She winked back at him.

"It's a *habit*, not a dress," I said all uppity like.

"Yeah, just don't get in the *habit* of wearing a *dress*," Keith said.

He and the sisters all cracked up.

I rolled my eyes.

I didn't know where we were going. Or how long it would take. But I *did* know one thing: This was going to be a *loooong* trip.

CHAPTER

9

"So where are we headed?" Diane asked Sister Mona.

"You don't even know where you're headed?" Sister Mona asked us. She looked shocked.

The train whistle blew, and the doors closed.

We lurched forward as the train started.

I bumped into Sister Clara. She was a tiny little woman. But I just found out she was built pretty solid. Her looks were deceiving. "Sorry," I said to her.

"Don't worry about it," she said back.

"So where *are* we headed?" Beth asked.

"Yeah, and will I be able to get back in time for dinner?" Keith asked. "If I don't get back in time for dinner, my mother goes nuts."

"Well," I said, "not if you call her."

Keith nodded. "Yeah, that's true."

Sister Mona looked between Keith, Diane, Beth, and me. "Well, kids? Let me put it to you this way . . ." She took a cell phone out from beneath the folds of her habit. Then she handed it to Keith.

He looked blankly at her. He didn't understand what Sister Mona was trying to tell him.

I rolled my eyes and shook my head. "You'd better call home," I said to Keith.

"Why?" he asked me.

I sighed loudly.

"Because we're not going to be able to get home in time for dinner, you moron!" I shouted.

"Eh, eh, eh," Sister Mona said to me. She held

out one pointer finger and wiped her other one across it several times.

It was my mother's hand signal for "No, no, no." I hadn't seen it since I was, like, four years old.

"Sorry," I muttered to Keith.

It looked like I'd better watch my mouth around these ladies. Especially Sister Mona.

Keith started dialing.

"Um, Mom? Yeah. I won't be home for dinner. I'm going to be at Al's tonight studying." He looked at me. "A sleepover? I'm not sure."

I nodded my head at Keith. "To be safe," I whispered.

"Oh. Mom? Yeah. To be safe. Let's just say it's a sleepover."

I smacked Keith.

"I mean, to be safe about whether we'll finish studying on time. Not to be safe about, well . . . anything else."

He was messing up totally. And was sounding shady.

I looked at Keith and slid my finger across my neck. It was our signal to say, "Cut it off. Now."

"Um, Mom? I've gotta go. Yeah. Don't worry. Yes, I have my own toothbrush there." Keith rolled his eyes.

I hit him again.

"I mean here. I have my own toothbrush *here*," he said into the phone.

He hung up.

"Well, *that* was smooth," I said to Keith. Of course, I was being sarcastic.

I half expected Sister Mona to say something about my comment. But she didn't. Instead, she nodded and said, "I can't believe your mother bought that."

Keith shrugged.

Sister Mona looked at me.

"Let's just say the acorn didn't fall far from the tree," I explained.

Sister Mona nodded and smiled. "I guess," was all she said.

Keith handed Sister Mona her phone. She slid it back underneath her habit.

For a second, I wondered what else was under there. Pots? Pans? A bag of chocolate chip cookies? Or maybe fruit?

Sister Mona looked like a fruit-eating kind of nun.

"So are we ever going to find out where we're going?" Beth asked loudly.

She'd interrupted my thoughts. And if you asked me, she was being a little rude. Okay, a lot rude. But Sister Mona didn't seem to mind.

"We're going to a retreat in the mountains. This is an express train. We'll get there in about four hours, Your Highness," Sister Mona said.

I laughed. *Your Highness*. Very funny. Beth *was* acting like spoiled royalty. Ever since we saw that movie.

The weird thing was that Beth didn't get Sister Mona's joke. Instead, she just nodded her head regally. Like she actually *was* a real princess or something.

"We should all take some seats," Sister Mona said. "This is going to take a while."

We followed her to the seating area and shuffled around. Switching places as we decided who should sit where.

That took a good fifteen minutes.

We finally ended up with me and Beth seated together facing forward, and Keith and Diane sitting together facing us. It was a special seating area in the middle of the train car. There were only two such areas where four people could sit facing one another.

Sister Mona and Sister Clara were across the aisle from us. They had the same seat setup.

But they were the only two in the seats. So they ended up putting their feet up on the seats across from them.

I looked at the nuns and smiled. They looked like reclining penguins.

I would have thought that was a sin or something. You know, putting your dirty shoes on the furniture.

The way my mother always yelled at me, you'd think it was.

Obviously, it wasn't.

But that had reminded me. "Sister Mona? May I call my mom?"

She reached into her habit and pulled out her phone. She held it out to me.

I got up from my seat and took it. "Thanks," I said to Sister Mona.

She just nodded silently.

I dialed home.

My mom answered after the third ring. "Hey, Mom?"

"Oh hi, dear," she said.

"Look. Keith and I are working on a project for school. Things aren't going as fast as we thought they would. Is it okay if I stay over here tonight?" I asked.

I liked that whole "over here" part. That made it seem like I was over at Keith's.

"Sure, honey," my mom said.

Good. That was easy.

"What's that noise?" she asked.

Uh-oh. "What noise?" I asked.

"It sounds like you're on a train," she said.

I laughed nervously. "A train?" I repeated to buy some time.

Sister Mona waved her hands to get my attention. She made the time-out signal. You know the one: one hand straight up and down, and the other across the top. Like a "T."

Then she held both of her hands out at an angle with her wrists touching. It looked like the letter "V."

Oh. I got it. "T-V." "We're just watching TV," I said to my mom.

"Well, maybe you'd get your work done faster if you turned off the TV," she said.

I didn't want her to think I was coming home anytime soon. So I said, "It's a great show. About the railroad. You know, an educational show," I said. "On PBS."

She loved shows like that. Couldn't resist them.

So I figured that would be a good excuse to have the TV on. And of course would also draw out our time to do our "project."

"That sounds good. What channel?" she asked.

Oh, no. This wasn't good. Now *she* wanted to watch it.

"Oh, wait a minute. It's not on PBS. Keith's telling me it's a video," I said.

I saw Sister Mona's eyebrows raise.

If I wasn't going to hell for all the *other* stuff I'd done, I knew I was going to hell for lying to my mother like this. I mean, *this* time, I had a witness. Sister Mona.

And as far as I knew, she had a direct line to the guy who could send me there in an instant. She probably spoke to him daily. And if he wasn't paying attention to me before, he sure was going to now!

Great.

"Mom, look. I've got to go. Keith's waiting for me. This project isn't going to do itself, you know," I said.

"Okay, dear. I'll plan on your staying at Keith's for the night. But if you want to come home earlier, just call and I'll come and get you."

"Okay. Thanks," I said.

"I love you," she trilled.

I rolled my eyes. "Yeah. Okay. Back at ya," I said. She liked it when I said stuff like that.

My mom always gets weird when I'm away for the night. She gets a little clingy. So I have to say stuff like that to calm her down.

I heard her click off the phone. Then I pushed the button on the cell phone to end the call.

Sister Mona kept resting there with her eyes closed.

I expected her to say something to me, but she didn't. Instead, she said, "Diane? Don't you have to call home too?"

Diane took the phone and then walked to the front end of the train car. I guess she wanted privacy to lie to her mother.

That was a *much* better idea then lying in front of a couple of nuns.

I wished *I* had thought of that. Oh, well. Too late.

Diane came back quickly and returned Sister Mona's phone.

Then she plopped down into her seat again.

"So what do we do now?" I asked my friends.

Everyone shrugged.

"Who knows?" Diane said.

"Do you know who those guys were?" I asked Beth.

"They could be anyone."

That was a stupid answer.

"They *were* 'anyone,'" I said. "I want to know who they actually *were*. And why they were after you."

Beth nodded. "I guess I owe you that," she said softly.

"Ya think?" Keith asked. "We almost got our butts shot off, and you 'guess' you owe us an explanation?"

Beth looked at Keith and me. "You mean you really don't know?"

"Know what?" we asked.

"Who I am?"

I shrugged. "You're Beth Smith."

"Yeah," Keith said.

Sister Mona laughed loudly.

She started hacking and coughing like crazy. She sounded like she was about to spew out a wad of something totally gross.

In fact, she sounded like she was going to die any second.

I was just about to perform the Heimlich on her.

But then she stopped. So I didn't have to.

Which was a good thing. Because I think it's a sin to hug a nun. Even if you're just, you know, Heimliching her.

"You okay?" I asked her.

"Yes, yes," she said. "It's just so funny."

"What's so funny?" I asked her.

"That you boys don't know Beth's a princess."

"What?!" Keith and I asked in unison.

CHAPTER

10

I looked at Beth.

She nodded.

So, she wasn't delusional?

I looked at Diane.

When she also nodded, I knew Sister Mona wasn't fooling around.

I looked at Beth again. "You're a princess."

"Yes."

"And you go to my school," I said.

"Yes."

"Whaddaya, own the town?" Keith asked her.

Beth looked at Keith. "No. A small country."

I looked from Beth to Diane to Sister Mona to Keith. "Well, that explains a lot."

I don't know why I said that. Because it really didn't explain anything.

"So why are people after you?" I asked Beth.

"There's a group of crazy radicals. They're trying to take over my country by force."

"But why do they want you?" I asked her.

"Probably as leverage," Sister Mona said. "So Beth's father will walk away easily."

I stared at Sister Mona. "How do you know all that?" I asked her.

She scoffed. "Don't you read the newspaper?" she asked me.

I shrugged. "The comics. Sometimes."

I felt like an idiot.

"So you never knew who I was?" Beth asked me.

I shook my head. "No, sorry."

Diane snorted with disgust. "How could you *not* know who she is, Al? She *wants* everyone to treat her like she's just a normal kid, and we all do that for her, but she *is* a princess!" Diane rolled her eyes at me like I was a real moron.

"Shouldn't *you* call someone?" Sister Mona said to Beth.

Beth shrugged. "Well, I could call Mrs. Holt."

Keith gasped. "Mrs. Holt's your *mother*?"

Then he had another thought. "Wait a minute. *You're* a princess, and your mother's working as a school *lunch lady*?"

He looked horrified.

"No, Keith," Beth said as she rolled her eyes and sighed loudly.

"Mrs. Holt is Beth's bodyguard," Diane explained.

"Ohhh," he said, and nodded.

"Why'd they make her a *lunch* lady?" I asked.

"I wanted to live like a normal kid for once," Beth said.

"And as a lunch lady? She'd have a reason to be near Beth without it looking too . . . secret service-y," Diane explained.

That *did* sort of make sense.

"Yeah, you should call her," I told Beth. "She's real worried about you."

Beth nodded.

"Her number ends with a seven," I said.

She shot me a weird look. "I know."

Beth took the phone and told Mrs. Holt where we were and where we were headed.

Once she got off the phone, things got kind of boring.

"How much longer till we get there?" Beth asked Sister Mona.

"A while, child. A while," she said calmly.

Sister Mona's eyes were still closed and she was very still. Her body was rocking side to side with the movement of the train. But she reached into her habit and pulled something out.

She held it toward us.

Since I was closest to Sister Mona, I took whatever she was holding out.

I looked at it. It was an iPod.

Cool!

Beth grabbed it from my hand. "I'll take that," she said with a sigh.

I looked over at Sister Mona. She still hadn't moved. But she was now wearing a little smile across her face.

"Have a TV in there?" I asked Sister Mona.

She laughed. "No, but I have a splitter. And another set of ear buds, if you and Beth want to share the iPod."

I looked at Beth. She didn't look like she wanted to share. "No thanks, Sister. That's okay."

Sister Mona nodded. Her eyes were still closed.

Before she could fall asleep again, I asked, "Got any food in there?"

It was getting late, and I was getting hungry.

Hey, I'm a growing boy. I seem to eat everything and anything lately. I get hungry often.

Sister Mona said nothing, and I thought she was already asleep. But then she reached into her habit and took out a long loaf of bread.

She handed it to me across the aisle.

"Gee, thanks," I said. I broke off a piece and started eating.

"Want some cheese with that?" Sister Clara asked. She pulled something out from underneath *her* habit.

Wow. It was a whole wheel of cheese. In a big Ziploc bag. Cool!

"Anyone have a root beer?" I called out.

Of course I was just joking! But lo and behold, not ten seconds later, a can of root beer soda was passed to me from the back of the train car.

"Anybody packing ice?" I asked aloud.

The nuns all laughed at that one. I guess it *would* be a little uncomfortable carrying ice under one's habit.

But on the other hand, how comfortable could it

be carrying around a whole wheel of cheese—or a loaf of bread—under there?

I waited a good twenty seconds to see if any ice would be coming forth, but . . . nope. No ice.

CHAPTER

11

We all sat around and talked and stuff. It took a while, but the train finally got to wherever we were going.

Sister Mona and Sister Clara led us off the train.

"Just follow us," Sister Mona said as we got off with the rest of the nuns in our train car.

Once we got off, I looked around. Boy, was I shocked.

The platform—no, the entire train station—was wall-to-wall nuns!

They were everywhere!

I'd thought there were a lot of nuns in the train car on the ride up. But that was *nothing* compared with the amount of nuns at the station.

The entire train must've been *filled* with nuns.

Not just in our car. But every car!

If we'd had on regular clothes, we would have stuck out like sore thumbs. Sister Mona was smart to tell us to stay in the habits. Because we blended in perfectly. We got lost in the sea of tuxedo dresses.

"Do you have any luggage you need help with, Sisters? Or do you guys carry everything under there," I said. I was pointing to Sister Mona's stomach area.

Sister Mona laughed. "Yes, Al, we *do* use luggage. But don't worry about it. It will be unloaded for us and put into our rooms at the inn."

"We don't have any luggage," Keith said. "And we don't have any rooms at the inn." Then he laughed. "I guess that means we have rooms at the 'out.' Get it? We don't have rooms at the 'in,' so we have rooms at the 'out'?"

I almost whacked him, but Sister Mona spoke up. "Yes, Keith. We get it," she said.

I looked at her. "You have the patience of a saint!" I said. Then I realized what I'd said and laughed.

"You must too," she said as she laughed with me.

We both looked at Keith.

He was looking around and didn't hear a word we'd said. As usual, he was totally out of it.

"Do you think I'll get extra points for being his best friend?" I asked her.

I was talking about, you know, the big picture. Yeah, I lied to my mother. Yeah, I wasn't a great student. Yeah, I didn't always do the right thing. But . . . I stuck with Keith. No matter what. That ought to count for *something*!

"I'm thinking you probably will," Sister Mona said to me. She looped her arm across my shoulders, and we started walking.

"So how far away is the inn?" Beth asked.

Her shoes weren't the best for hiking around mountains. They were high heeled and had little straps. Pretty. But not too practical.

"Only about a quarter mile more," Sister Mona said.

"Will you make it?" I asked Beth.

She shot me a look. "Of *course* I'll make it."

We got to the inn, and I was thankful that we walked right to the dining hall. I was hungry again.

"Welcome, Sisters," our waiter said.

He gave me a double take when it was my turn to give my order.

His face showed a little disgust, but then he tried to hide it and smiled at me. "And what can I get for you, Sister?" he asked me.

Keith cracked up.

The waiter noticed Keith and was again repulsed by what he saw.

Yeah, I know. We were two butt-ugly nuns.

Keith was even showing signs of a future mustache. Me? I still had lightish peach fuzz. But Keith? He was . . . well, not a very pretty woman.

I was hungry, so I ordered just about everything on the special menu.

Keith ordered two main dishes and three desserts.

So we wouldn't feel bad, Sister Clara changed her order to include two more desserts. And then Sister Mona ordered two extra servings of French fries. "I *love* French fries. They're my weakness. But I don't have them often," she said to us after the waiter left.

"French fries are a sin?" I asked. Oh, my God! If French fries were a sin, I was on the express line to hell!

"Oh no, no, no, my child. French fries aren't a sin. But I have health problems. So I shouldn't eat them."

Whew. That took a load off! "That's great!" I said without thinking. Then my brain kicked in.

"I mean about the French fries. Not about your health problems."

Sister Mona nodded. "I figured that's what you meant, Al."

After dinner, we had to go to a retreat meeting.

"Do we *have* to go?" Keith whined.

I looked at Sister Mona. I really didn't want to go either.

"Yes, I'm sorry. It's compulsory," she said.

I didn't know what that meant, but I *did* understand that we had to go. And if you have to go, you have to go.

And speaking of which, I had to go. "I'll be right back," I said.

I headed for the men's room, but Sister Mona grabbed me by the back of the habit.

She shook her head and then looked at the ladies' room door.

"You're kidding me, right?" I asked her.

She looked at my habit. "No," she said.

Oh, God. I had *no* desire to see naked nuns.

"Maybe I should go up to the room," I said.

Sister Mona nodded. "Good choice."

"Yeah, and I'll join ya," Keith said.

I guess he didn't want to see anything gross either.

"We'll wait," Sister Mona said.

"No, that's okay," I said. "Go on ahead without us."

I figured if they went to the meeting, and we went to the room, we could cut out of most of the meeting. Maybe all of it.

Sister Clara laughed. "We weren't born yesterday, boys. We'll wait for you."

Okay. So they had us.

These nuns were smarter than I thought.

"Oh, all right," I said with a sigh. "We'll be right back."

CHAPTER

12

When we were alone in the room, I turned to Keith. "This is weird, huh?"

"Yeah, a little," Keith said as he straightened out his habit. He was standing in front of the mirror and looking at himself.

He obviously liked what he saw because he said, "You know, I always thought I looked good in a suit. But if you ask me, I look *really* good in this."

"Yeah, well, no one asked you. So keep your freaky thoughts to yourself, okay?"

Keith turned to the side to see himself from that view. He smiled and nodded. "Yeah, man. I'm looking *good*!"

"Sometimes, you worry me, dude," I said to Keith. "And I've got enough to worry about."

"Oh, yeah? Like what?" he asked me.

I couldn't believe my ears. "Like *what*?" I yelled. "How about the fact that we're upstate, God knows where! Because *I* don't know where we are. Do *you*?"

Keith shrugged. "No."

"We're stuck spending the night with a whole *lot* of nuns!" I screamed.

"Well, they're not going to hurt us," Keith said.

I shook my head. That wasn't the point! "Now add to that that we're here with two girls—one of which is a *princess*," I tried to explain.

"Yeah? So? She won't hurt us either."

I'd been on the edge of losing it and now I was hurtling over the edge. "Are you forgetting the guys who were *after* her? The men *shooting* at us, you nimrod?" I bellowed.

Keith looked surprised. "You know, I was having such a good time, I *did* forget about them."

Just as my hands were reaching for his neck, the door burst open.

"Are you ladies ready to go?" Diane said with a roll of her eyes. "Sister Mona doesn't want to be late."

I stormed out of the room and kept quiet. If Keith said another word, his life would be in danger. From *me*!

We got to the meeting room just as the doors were shutting. We were the last ones in.

Some really old, pruney-looking nun was standing at the front of the room.

"As always, we would like to start off this session by having each of us speak our favorite verse from the Bible. But this time we will not start in front. Instead, we will start from the back row."

I looked around. You'll never guess who was in the back row.

That's right. Us.

As luck would have it, Sister Mona went first. She said something nice. I liked it.

Then Sister Clara went. Hers was nice too.

I was racking my brain, trying to think if I knew a verse from the Bible. But I couldn't think of one. Not one.

It was Keith's turn next. I watched him to see what he would say.

I figured that whatever he said, I could just say, "Oh, dang! That was *my* favorite too!"

I did that a lot in school. I mean, how could your teacher *prove* that it wasn't your favorite? Or that the guy before you didn't just steal your answer?

I was almost in the clear when I heard Keith speak.

"In God we trust," he said.

What?! That was the stupidest thing I'd ever heard!

I may not know the Bible or anything. But I *knew* that was from the dollar bill.

"That's on *money*, you idiot. It's not in the *Bible!*" I pelted him across the chest. Between this and the whole "forgetting we got shot at" thing, I was ready to shoot him myself.

"It's not?" he asked. "You'd figure it *would* be."

"Well, it's not, you moron!" I couldn't help myself. I was yelling.

Loud enough for all to hear.

"You'll have to excuse Sister, um, Keisha . . . and, um, Sister Al . . . vina. They're new," Sister Mona said to the crowd of surprised faces.

I looked at Sister Mona. Sister *Alvina*? That was the best she could come up with?

Keith laughed. "Sister Alvina," he said. "That's funny." He was all bent over in his little nun outfit, laughing his butt off.

"Shut up, Sister *Keisha*." I couldn't stop myself. I belted him again.

Keith was still bent over laughing, but he

managed to turn around and head-butt me in the stomach.

There was a loud group gasp from the meeting room.

I guess the nuns weren't used to seeing two of their sisters going at it like a World Wrestling Federation SmackDown.

"I'm sorry, Sisters. I think they're a little light-headed from the altitude," Sister Mona said as she grabbed us by the back of our habits and pushed us toward the back door.

"Yeah, I'm more than a little sick of *his* altitude!" I said as we cleared the room.

Sister Clara, Beth, and Diane were right behind us.

"It's altitude, Al. Not attitude," Diane said.

"Whatever," I said. "I'm just sick of him."

"Look, boys," Sister Mona said. "You're under a lot of stress. I understand that. But you have to keep your wits."

"I *have* all my wits," I said as I pulled myself out

of her grasp and smoothed out my habit. "*He*"—I pointed to Keith—"only has half."

Beth giggled. "That's funny. I get it. You just called him a half-wit."

"Look, guys," Diane said. "We need to stick together."

"That's right," Sister Mona said. "The retreat ends tomorrow night. So you will be on your own by then."

I looked at Sister Mona.

"I'd love to take you back to the convent, Al. But I *know* that's not allowed," she said.

"Look. Let's all go to bed. It's late, we're tired. And tomorrow morning we'll make a plan," Diane said.

She was right. There was nothing else we could do tonight.

CHAPTER

13

The next morning, we were all up early.

"I'm reading a great book," Sister Clara said. "And I only have ten pages left."

"Do you want to finish it and meet us down at the dining room?" Sister Mona asked her.

"That would be great," she said.

We walked down to the dining room.

"After breakfast, you can plan what you'll do," Sister Mona said to Beth, Diane, Keith, and me.

We had the same waiter we'd had last night.

Only this time, he was looking at me funny.

Not grossed-out funny, but weird funny. Like he was looking to see if I matched a picture or something.

Then he looked at Keith.

Once again, unlike last night, he wasn't repulsed by how ugly Keith was as a nun. Instead, he looked at Keith hard. Then nodded his head and smiled.

He looked at Sister Mona. Then shifted his eyes toward Diane and Beth. When his eyes hit on Beth, they sparkled.

I thought I heard the sound *ka-ching*. You know, like a cash register. But maybe it was only in my mind.

"I'll be right back with your food," the waiter said. "Don't go anywhere," he added.

He rushed off to the kitchen, looking back at us quickly. Twice.

"How can he be right back with our food?" Keith asked. "He never took our orders."

Dang. This couldn't be good.

Just then Sister Clara rushed in.

"You kids need to leave. Right now. Start running and don't look back. You hear?" she said to us.

"What's the matter?" Sister Mona asked her.

"On my way in, I overheard our waiter from last night. He was on the phone. He said, 'Yeah, it's them. Four kids. Two girls, two boys. And I recognized the princess from those *People* magazine photos.' Then he said something *really* awful," Sister Clara said.

"What?" we all asked.

"He asked if he was going to get the money."

"What does *that* mean?" Keith asked.

"It means we've got a price on our heads, you moron!" I shouted.

"We've got to get out of here," Beth said. "Now!"

She was right.

"What about breakfast?" Keith asked.

"Sorry, no time," I said to him as I got up from my chair.

Sister Mona jumped up and flew to the next

table. She swiped the food right off some plates and all but threw it as us. "Sorry," she said to the startled nuns at the table. "I'll explain later."

"Eww, pancakes," Keith said as one slapped him on the cheek. "Thanks."

Sister Mona tossed waffles at Beth, Diane, and me like Frisbees.

"Okay, now go! Head north," Sister Mona said.

"But we live south," I argued.

"That's why you need to head north. No one will look for you that way."

"Yeah," I said. "And we won't get *home* that way either!"

"You need to head north, Al. Please. Trust me. If you head south, you'll run into great danger."

We headed north.

We were walking as fast as we could, still in our nun's habits. Only this time, without our street clothes underneath, because the inn was a bit stuffy and we were planning on staying there all day.

"How do you think they found us?" I said aloud.

I wasn't really asking anyone, just talking to myself.

"I have no clue," Beth said.

"First they found us at the mall," I said.

"And then they found out where we were staying," Diane added.

"Yeah," I said. "How'd they *do* that?"

"Who knew we were at that inn?" Diane asked. "I didn't tell my parents. Did you?"

"No," Keith said. "They think I'm at Al's."

"Mine think I'm at Keith's," I said.

We stared at Beth.

"I told Mrs. Holt we caught up with this band of traveling nuns," she said. "I told her we left from track B on the express train."

"She must have found out where the train was headed," Diane said.

"And where the nuns were staying," I added.

"Oh, my gosh!" Beth screamed. "Maybe they got

to her. Maybe they tortured her to find out where I am."

Beth grabbed my arm.

"I need to call her," she wailed. "If she got hurt because of me, I'll never forgive myself."

We kept walking until we came to a little house.

"Maybe they'll let me use their phone," Beth said.

We knocked on the door, and a lady answered.

"Are you kids okay?" she asked. Then she saw the nuns outfits and seemed confused.

"May we use your phone, please?" Beth asked her.

She took out her big wad of cash and peeled off a hundred-dollar bill. Then she passed it to the woman.

"Your money is not good here, Princess," the lady said with a smile.

What?! Did *everyone* except Keith and me know she's a princess?

She took us to her phone, where Beth called Mrs. Holt.

Beth nodded to us when Mrs. Holt must've answered.

"Are you okay?" Beth asked her frantically.

Then Beth's eyes bulged out, and she quickly turned and slammed down the phone.

"What's the matter?" Diane asked.

"What happened?" I asked.

"She asked why I left the inn," Beth said.

"So?" Keith asked.

"So," I said. "How did she know that Beth *left* the inn?"

Keith's face was blank.

"Unless *she* was the one who was paying off the inn's staff to let her know where Beth was?" I finished, so Keith could get with the program.

"Ohhh," Keith said.

"Oh, no!" I said.

"What?" Beth asked.

"*I'm* the one who told her we were at the mall!" I said.

"So *that's* how they found us," Diane said.

I felt terrible.

"But I thought she was your bodyguard. Why would she tell the bad guys where you were?" I asked Beth.

"She must have been bought off. The rebels have a lot of money," was all she said.

She looked sad.

I guess if I'd been double-crossed by someone I'd trusted, I'd look sad too.

"Now what?" Keith asked.

CHAPTER
14

We'd stayed in our nuns habits to stay under-cover.

But now our enemy knew of our disguise.

"Do you have clothes that will fit us?" I asked the lady.

"Yes," she said. "I'll bring you boys some of my husband's clothes. You girls can wear mine."

As soon as we changed, we said good-bye to the nice lady.

We didn't want to involve her in this mess.

"I slipped some money under her lamp to say thank you," Beth said as we hiked along the road. "Do you think six hundred will cover it?"

Keith stopped walking. "For *four* outfits? That's like . . ." he paused to calculate. "One hundred fifty an outfit."

"Yes? So?" Diane said.

"Who spends one hundred fifty dollars on an *outfit*?" he howled.

Beth looked at Keith and then at me. "You don't?"

Keith snorted a laugh. "Have you *seen* the way Al dresses?"

"Hey," I said. "Keep me out of this."

We started walking again, but ran into a little problem. Or, should I say, the little problem flew our way.

"Do you hear that?" I asked anyone who'd answer.

"That whirring noise?" Diane asked.

"Yeah," I said. "That's the one."

I looked up.

Just great!

I mean, really. Who can outrun a helicopter?

I can't even outrun a three-legged dog!

There we were. Walking along the twisting and turning mountain road. When out of the blue, sitting above us, is this massive helicopter.

It hovered over us awhile, and we were acting pretty cool about the whole thing. You know. Like people who weren't getting chased by killers would act.

Just walking along, minding our own business.

Keeping our heads down.

Then it sank lower, and a guy with a long gun with a scope on it started aiming at us.

All of a sudden we weren't just plain ol' kids walking down the road anymore.

We were four scared kids running like maniacs as some lunatic tried to pick us off with a high-powered rifle!

"We're getting shot at, Al," Keith said.

"I *know* we're getting shot at, Keith!" I shouted over the noise of the rifle and the helicopter.

"I don't like getting shot at," he shouted.

"It's not my favorite thing either, bud," I shouted back.

I *really* was not in the mood for any of this.

I was tired, cranky, and getting shot at.

Then it hit me. My most horrible thought ever!

I actually wished I were back at school!

Oh God, take me now! I think I'm ready for you!

Today—the day I wished I were at school—was a day worth dying.

"Would you shut up, Al? And keep running!" Keith said.

Had I said anything? Had I said it out loud? "I didn't say anything," I shouted over the racket.

"Yes, you did, Al. You're crying like a girl and begging God to 'come get me now,'" Keith said.

"I said that out loud?" I asked.

"A few times," Diane shouted my way. "I think, like, seven."

"Thanks for counting," I said to her.

All of a sudden, Beth slowed down and started to wheeze.

"What's the matter?" I asked her.

"I'm tired of running. I can't keep up," she said.

"Look," I said, "you *have* to keep running! Just relax. And breathe," I said.

I always forgot to breathe when I was running the track at school. Coach White always said to me, "Breathe, you girly-man," as I wheezed by him. So I thought I'd share Coach White's wisdom now.

"Just relax and breathe," I said to Beth again.

"Don't tell me to breathe!" she said.

She looked ticked. At me.

Let me get this straight: I just changed out of a nun's outfit. I'm running my butt off. In the middle of nowhere. Getting chased by a lunatic in a helicopter. While he's shooting at me. All because of her. And she's ticked off at *me*?

Future queen or not, she had *no* right to be mad at *me*!

"I'll breathe if I *want* to breathe!" she spat out. "And I don't *want* to breathe!"

I was running my legs off. Running for my life. But I still managed to roll my eyes. "That's very mature," I said to her.

"And don't you roll your eyes at *me*!" she screamed. "I can be as mature or as *not* mature as I want to be!"

She was hysterical now.

Great.

Just what I needed.

I couldn't help it. My eyes rolled again.

"You did it *again*!" she screamed. "How *dare* you!"

Well, at least she was breathing again. You had to breathe to scream at someone, didn't you? I *thought* you did.

"Look, I don't know about you, but I'm going to keep my butt moving," I shouted at her.

Was it me? Or did it get noisier?

I looked up to see another helicopter overhead, shooting at the first helicopter.

"Stop running, kids, and take cover," someone said from the second helicopter.

Oh, great. We were going to have a spraying shootout of bullets overhead.

Yeah. That was good.

Just then a *really* loud machine gun from the latest helicopter started shooting at the first helicopter. "Oh, he's going *down*!" I said.

"Who's going down?" Keith asked as we started to slow down and run into the woods.

"The jerk shooting at us," I said.

Just as I said that, I saw the guy who was shooting at us fall out of his helicopter. We watched as he landed with a thud.

"Good!" I said to the new guys. "Go bring down the whole bird!" I shouted.

As if they'd listened to me, the aircraft that was first after us started spinning. Black smoke was spiraling up out of the front of the helicopter.

"Get out of the way, kids," someone said to us from the second bird. I think they were afraid the helicopter would get out of control.

I watched as the first helicopter's pilot was shot. Right in the forehead! Then he slumped over his controls. After that, the second helicopter brought out the big artillery. They shot off a huge, missile-like thing. It blew that first helicopter to *bits*!

Pieces were raining down around us. There was smoke and ashes *everywhere*.

Cop cars were flying up the mountain roads. They were coming from both directions.

Another chopper flew overhead. So now there were two again.

In the distance, I could see fighter planes whizzing toward us.

"You kids okay?" someone asked from the helicopter that saved our butts.

We were all in a bit of shock, I guess. Because no one answered. We were just standing there like big dummies.

"Give us a thumbs-up if you're okay," a man said from the newly arrived helicopter.

I could have sworn I saw Mrs. Holt in that one. But I wasn't sure.

CHAPTER
15

We all gave a thumbs-up. Everyone was okay.

"Go with the police. They'll take you home," the guy on the chopper's PA system said.

We all piled into the only police car that would fit all of us. Every other police unit had two officers in it. This car only had one.

Keith got in front, and Diane, Beth, and I went in the back.

Everything looked normal. At least at first glance.

But then I needed to pull over. You know, to "go."

The officer had to get out of the car to open our door for us. I never would have thought about that. But it seems you can't get out of a police car's backseat from the inside. I guess they don't want criminals just leaving or something.

Anyhow, he had to get out to let me out, so I could, um, you know.

That's when I noticed.

His pants were too tight and too short. And his shirt was also too tight.

I know that doesn't *seem* like anything strange. We all know how old people have no style. We're used to seeing them wearing all *sorts* of weird things. But this guy was a cop. He needed to move around. Needed freedom to run and shoot. I couldn't see a cop wanting tight clothes.

After I did my thing, I came back to the car.

I sat in the backseat trying to figure out what

would happen next. If this guy wasn't a cop, that could only mean he was something else.

At the moment, "something else" was a bad thing. I could feel it in my bones.

"That was cool the way that gunner fell to his death, wasn't it, Al?" Keith asked.

I watched the cop. His face tightened.

"Not really," I said. "He was a person."

I was hoping the "cop" driving us home would take it easy on us if he thought we were, you know, nice people.

"And wasn't it cool the way the pilot got it in the head?" Keith asked.

Great. Tick off the guy who's in charge of our lives, Keith! "No, dude," I said. "It wasn't cool. It was very, very *un*cool!" I said loudly.

I hoped the guy heard me.

He did, because I saw him nod very slightly.

We'd gone about fifteen miles and I figured I could stop again.

"Um, Officer? I need to go again," I said. I made

a face that I hoped showed how badly I had to go.

"Again?" he asked. He was not a happy camper.

"Yeah," I said. "Sorry."

The "cop" pulled over.

"Can we stop at a rest stop?" I asked. I was hoping for a crowded place. You know, with people, or a phone, or other *real* cops.

"No. You'll go here," he said gruffly.

I walked into the woods. "Great," I said to myself.

There were no big limbs lying around. Nothing I could use to knock out the bad guy.

There was a little twig lying nearby.

Maybe I can poke his eye out, I thought.

Yeah, right.

I looked at the tree I was, um, watering.

I reached up, hoping to break off the limb.

It was too high. I had to jump.

I jumped about as well as I ran.

But, again, my life depended upon it. So I jumped again. This time I reached the limb.

I was hanging there. Just dangling from the tree limb.

I wiggled, trying to break off the limb.

Nothing. It didn't break.

I wiggled some more.

"Hey, kid," the guy shouted. "What *are* you doing?"

"I'm a little stiff," I said. "I thought I'd do some pull-ups."

I heard Keith laugh. "That's funny. Al doing pull-ups."

Great. There he goes, blowing my cover again.

"Get back to the car, kid. And stop fooling around," the guy said. He was getting angry. I could tell.

I fell from the limb and walked back to the car.

Everyone was looking at me like I was nuts.

"That was funny, Al," Keith said from the front seat. "You can't do a pull-up in gym class. What makes you think you can do some now? The fresh mountain air?" He laughed his head off.

"Would you shut up?" I snapped. "I can do a pull-up in gym class."

"Maybe *one*," Keith laughed. "But not two in a row."

I looked at the girls. "Just shut up, Keith. Okay?" I begged.

"Why don't you *all* shut up?" the bad guy ordered.

I think my friends finally caught on to what was going on.

"He's not very friendly," Diane whispered.

"I thought all American police officers were supposed to be friendly," Beth said.

"He's not a cop," I whispered.

Beth stiffened. "Then who is he?" she whispered back.

"I don't know. But I *do* know he's not a cop."

We drove in silence for another fifteen or twenty minutes.

"Um, Officer?" I said, "I have to go again."

He went ballistic and slammed on the brakes.

We skidded to a halt.

"I don't know which one of you I want to kill first," he said. He pulled out his gun.

We gasped.

"*You*," he said, and pointed his gun at Keith. "You're an idiot! And a huge pain in the neck!"

Keith looked offended.

"And *you*." He pointed his gun at Diane. "Your voice gets on my nerves."

Now she looked offended too.

"And *you*," he said as he pointed his gun at Beth. "With you out of the way, I'll finally have the power I deserve!"

He looked happy. Beth didn't.

"And you? The kid with the bladder problem?" He waved his gun at me. "I just want to shoot you to put you out of your misery," he said. "You must have a bladder the size of a thimble!"

Then he laughed. A mean, weird laugh.

He sounded like the villain he was.

And a touch insane.

"Like I said," he said, "I don't know which one of you I want to kill first."

He made everyone get out at gunpoint.

"I really need to go," I said. "But it's number two this time. Have any toilet tissue?"

He rolled his eyes. "What are you? Some kind of human waste machine?"

I shrugged.

"There are a couple of napkins on the dash-board," Keith said. Then he laughed. "From a doughnut shop. Get it?"

The guy was a bad guy. And not a real cop. But if he *were* real? Keith would've managed to tick him off by now too.

"Just get the damn napkins," the guy said to me.

I whispered to Beth, "Keep him busy. And keep his back to me. Okay?"

She made a face. "I'll try," she said.

She walked toward the woods. "Ow. I think I twisted my ankle in these shoes. Can you please help me, Officer?" she said sweetly.

"Let your friend help you," he said roughly. He was pointing the gun at Beth.

Diane walked slowly over to Beth. I saw Beth whisper to Diane.

In a flash, I was back with the police stick he'd left in the car.

I snuck up behind him and put my finger to my lips. I hoped everyone realized what I was going to do.

I aimed it at his head.

I was just about to swing. Hard!

But first I said, "Lucky for me, I don't have your problem. I know just who I want to kill first." I swung the club.

The cracking sound it made as it met the side of his head was loud. And solid.

He went down like a big ol' tree when a cartoon guy shouts, *"Timber!"*

He didn't know what hit him.

"And I *don't* have a bladder problem!" I said to his prone body.

Just then, Mrs. Holt came rushing out of one of the police cars that came barreling over to us. "He's not a cop!" she shouted as she ran toward us. Her gun was cocked and aimed our way.

"We figured that out," I said as I stepped in front of Beth like a human shield.

Mrs. Holt didn't know that we'd also figured out that it was *she* who'd sold us out. That she was a double agent.

Her gun moved to the guy lying in the leaves.

She looked at the guy and made a face. "Oh, bummer," she said. "You beat me to him."

"Sorry, "I said coolly. "If it makes you feel better, I don't think he's dead," I added.

She looked at me. "Hmm. I don't know if that makes me feel better."

She walked over to the guy and felt his neck. "Oh, good. He's still alive."

She smiled her strange smile.

While she was walking to him, I reached back and pushed Beth behind Keith.

Now she had two human shields.

Diane saw what we were doing, and she too stood blocking Beth from Mrs. Holt.

"Maybe you'll still have your chance to kill him," I said slowly. "But you won't get a chance to kill Beth."

She turned to look at us.

"Kill Beth?" she gasped. "I'd never kill Beth."

She started walking toward Beth.

"Don't kill me! *Please!*" Beth cried out.

It was time to show our cards.

"We figured out he wasn't a cop, and we also figured out that *you* sold us out."

"No, no," she said, shaking her head.

"Yes, yes," I replied.

"No," she demanded. "You don't understand. We had everything in place. I was only pretending that I was double-crossing you. It was our plan. My orders, really. We needed to find out just who, exactly, was behind this!"

She was pleading with us.

"I would never, *ever* hurt Beth. She is our future

queen! I am honored to be entrusted with her life."

"I don't believe you," Beth said.

Mrs. Holt—if that was even really her name—looked crushed.

"Please," she whispered. "Ask your father."

More people had arrived, and the bad guy was taken from his place on the ground.

"Your father wants to speak with you," a man said to Beth.

The four of us walked to the helicopter together, Beth in the middle and Keith, Diane, and I surrounding her.

At this point, we trusted no one.

Someone handed Beth the radio transmitter.

"Honey? Are you there?" a man said.

"Daddy?" she wailed. "Is that you?"

"Yes, Beth. It's me. Are you okay, honey?"

"Yes, but I think Mrs. Holt has gone to the other side."

She heard her father laugh. "Oh no, my child. It was all arranged that way. We are tired of our enemy's antics. We've had enough. We needed to flush them out. At first, your Mrs. Holt wouldn't even agree to do this. But we insisted."

We all looked at Mrs. Holt. She was crying.

"She was very afraid that this would not work out as we'd planned," Beth's father said. "But it did. And we are now safe. Our family, the country—we are all safe now. We've gotten them, child. You may come home now. I hear we owe great thanks to your American friends."

ONE LAST THING . . .

"I'm sorry you have to go home," I said to Beth.

"She must be with her people," her dad said to me. He put his arm around his daughter.

"Wow," I said. "You really *are* a princess."

"Yes," she said simply. "I'll someday be queen."

I nodded. "Sorry I didn't know that. I'll try to read the paper more."

The king laughed. Then he turned serious. "Thank you, Mr. Netti. You saved my daughter and my country," he said gravely. "My people and I cannot thank you enough for that. You have single-handedly saved Freitonia."

"You can call me Al, Mr., um, King. I mean, um, sir.

Or, um, Your Highness." I didn't really know how to talk to a king.

"Thank you . . . Al," he said. Then he bowed to me. Really low.

I didn't know what to do, so I did the same thing to him. I felt kind of silly, but when I looked at Beth, she was smiling and nodding.

"You did a fine job, Al," Mrs. Holt said. "Thank you."

"Your cover as a lunch lady was perfect," I said. "Next time you need to kill someone, just make them some lunch. Maybe some pudding for dessert," I suggested.

Mrs. Holt laughed. "Yes, I will. That ought to kill them for sure!"

Beth laughed at Mrs. Holt. "I don't think you'll miss that part of the assignment. You *really* were a bad cook." Then Beth giggled. "You'll probably get a better lunch lady now that she's leaving," she said to me.

"I won't hold my breath," I said. "Like I said, her cover was perfect. She'll most likely be replaced by another horrible cook."

Beth looked confused.

"It's an American lunch-lady tradition," I tried to explain.

The king looked at his watch. "It is time to leave," he said regally.

I looked at Beth and smiled. "It sure was fun," I said to her shyly.

"Yes, it was," she said a little sadly. "I *liked* being a regular person. It felt good. But duty calls, and now I have to go back to my country."

I didn't know what to say to that. So I just nodded and smiled.

"I will miss you, Al," she said softly.

"I'll miss you, too, Beth," I said back, and meant it.

The king cleared his throat loudly.

"Now that you have ridden Freitonia of my worst enemy, you are free to visit our country anytime, Al," he said to me. "Just say the word, and we will have a plane sent to get you."

Wow. Cool!